Giving an Inch

THE PROFESSOR'S RULE, #1

Heidi Belleau
Amelia C. Gormley

RIPTIDE
PUBLISHING

Riptide Publishing
PO Box 6652
Hillsborough, NJ 08844
www.riptidepublishing.com

Giving an Inch (The Professor's Rule, #1)
Copyright © 2013 by Heidi Belleau and Amelia C. Gormley

Cover Art by L.C. Chase, lcchase.com/design.htm
Editor: Rachel Haimowitz
Layout: L.C. Chase, lcchase.com/design.htm

ISBN: 978-1-62649-017-8

Second edition
September, 2013

Also available in ebook:
ISBN: 978-1-62649-016-1

Giving an Inch

THE PROFESSOR'S RULE, #1

Heidi Belleau
Amelia C. Gormley

RIPTIDE
PUBLISHING

J ames hated department stores. He hated the gleaming displays, hated the attractive salesgirls shilling wedding registries, hated the mannequins in their Tommy Hilfiger cashmere sweaters and leather loafers. Thousands, no, *millions* of dollars, all spent on multicolored stand mixers and designer purses and monogrammed fucking towels.

Mostly, though, he hated how being here made him feel like an out-of-touch slob. He didn't know the brands, didn't know what was in fashion. Hell, sometimes he didn't even know whether the shirt he was holding was meant for a woman or a man.

One of his old psych major friends would probably say he was transferring his anxiety about his Ph.D. program application over to the whole clothing issue, but the truth was that material culture—including technology and even basic pop culture—eluded James. Always had.

And his sister Carrie, who was way more up on these things than James could ever hope to be, had called up sick at the last minute, leaving him in the lurch. After a great deal of whining and pleading, she'd at least agreed to let him text her pictures of his various outfits, but that still left the issue of how he was supposed to *find* those outfits in the first place. Carrie, of course, thought he should just ask a salesperson, but James felt humiliated even doing that. After all, salespeople knew a thing or two about clothes. What would they think of James, in his threadbare old *Star Wars* T-shirt from the eighties and rotted canvas high-tops? Maybe that he was trying to steal something?

Or maybe that you're a hopelessly unfashionable dude who needs help picking out a suit for a professional presentation.

Too bad voices of reason were so very, very easily drowned out by the anxious swirl inside his head. You know, swirl, as in the motion of flushing something down the toilet?

He wandered from department to department, scowling at everything, fully expecting to be booted out by some manager who thought he was an aggressive homeless drug addict or something. And there came a man now, Indian with a dark complexion and a pin-neat tailored suit.

James put up his hands in surrender and was about to protest, "I'm going, I'm going," when the man said, "Can I help you find something, sir?"

Sir?

Was this dude seriously seeing the same James—ratty T-shirt, bad hair—that James himself saw in the mirror every morning?

A quick look over his shoulder confirmed that yes, the man was for some reason speaking to *him*. No other sirs here.

"Uh . . ." Well this was certainly a strange turn of events. James had already resigned himself to giving up altogether on the pretense of looking professional and just getting the hell out of there, but here he was getting exactly what he needed. "Yes?"

The salesman tilted his head with practiced patience.

Oh yes, this was the part where James told him what he wanted. Right. "Menswear?" James tried, palms sweating.

"You're in it," the salesman said, and gestured to either side of him, where racks upon racks of men's clothes stood waiting. Taunting James with their sheer fucking volume.

"Right. Okay. Um, I need . . ." *A suit? Is a suit too formal?* "I don't know what I need," he sighed at last, shoulders slumped in defeat.

The salesman chuckled, the sound not at all unkind. "How about we start with the basics, then? Are you shopping for a specific purpose or event? A job interview?" His accent was wonderful, lilting and precise, with a musicality that pleased the poet in James. ". . . A date?"

Wait, what was that tentativeness? Was he asking as a salesman, or as a *man*?

James stared at him, trying to translate the placid smile sketched across his face. Wow, he had full lips, and such a deep red-pink.

"Not a date," he said, perhaps a little too enthusiastically. "I'm single." Er, that definitely wasn't helping matters. James flailed a moment longer, then added, "I'm an academic, and I guess you could say it's an interview . . . of sorts. I'm doing my qualifying oral exam, which—oh, I guess you don't really care, do you? Anyway, there's going to be a panel of professors giving me the exam, people who are basically responsible for my future. So I guess it is an interview, just an interview for me to pay them and not the other way round." He laughed awkwardly, tucking his hands in his pockets before he started snapping his fingers or falling into one of his other incredibly annoying anxious tics.

When had he started up with those again? He thought he'd shed those habits four years ago.

"What are you studying?" the salesman asked.

"What?"

Nothing seemed to crack that patient, kind look. The salesman's eyes were liquid, so dark and mesmerizing. "What field of study are you going into for your Ph.D.?"

"Oh!" James said, flushing hot. "History. Lame, I know."

"Not at all!" The salesman smiled brightly. "It's a fascinating subject."

Jeeze, now the guy was just being *too* nice. "If you don't want a job when you graduate."

"I don't have a degree in anything, and yet, I have a job."

James, you asshole. "Bet you didn't have to go into as much debt as I did to get here."

The salesman's eyes twinkled. "That's true. So how about a nice pair of slacks and a buttoned shirt? Not a full suit, although I could certainly show you some tie and blazer options so you can mix and match. Can I get you in some elbow patches, perhaps?"

"Elbow patches? You got some kinda dusty academic fetish there, buddy? Because if that's the case, I've got an IKEA shelf just bursting with leather-bound books." He probably shouldn't have said that. *Get ahold of yourself, man. You're running off the rails.*

The salesman gave him a look that seemed to ride the line between scandalized and amused and possibly flirtatious. Which wasn't really a line so much as it was a Venn diagram. "Right. So. Shirts," he said, and disappeared into the endless racks of clothes.

The salesman assigned James a fitting room, then filled it with more shirts and trousers and blazers than he'd ever seen, much less worn. (Had he even known shirts could come in something other than scratchy polyester blend, let alone silk?) He'd expected a quick in and out: put on shirt, put on pants, snap picture, get a yes or no, move on. But instead, after he was dressed the salesman coaxed him out of the stall again and put him in front of a large, three-way mirror.

Can't get enough of me, huh buddy? The salesman certainly was handsy, but maybe James was just being an ass, assuming that the guy was doing anything other than his job, which apparently included fittings for alterations.

Around the time the salesman stood behind James and pinched the extra fabric at his hips, talking about tailoring and such, though, James began to think it wasn't so much "possibly" flirtatious as "definitely." Couldn't go too far, of course: had to be all professional and whatnot. He didn't do anything that James could make a complaint about if he were so inclined (which he most certainly was not), but the vibe was there, waiting for James to pick up on it.

The vibe was there and so were his hands, right on James's hips, and this shopping excursion was about to get *really* awkward if James was reading that vibe wrong.

Just how distracted did he want to let himself get, anyway? He was definitely on a mission; after all, the shopping *had* to be done. But could he manage to work his digits into the guy's cell phone before he left? Secure an invitation to coffee or dinner or whatever?

He pictured himself charming his way into the guy's pants with tales of Robert the Bruce. Not that geeking out about history had *ever* worked on a date before, but the salesman had been the one to call it fascinating first. Of course, that could just be flattery to make a sale.

Ugh, picking up guys was way too complicated in meatspace. Maybe the salesman had a Grindr app.

"Let me go grab some pins and a measuring tape," the salesman murmured, glancing down to where the hem of the slacks dragged on the floor several inches below James's ankles. "We can have them taken in a little at the hips and thighs as well as hemmed; a little bit of custom tailoring can take something off the rack and make it incredible."

James nodded, because "I have no idea what you're talking about" didn't seem like it would be all that charming. The salesman lingered just a second more before releasing his hips and disappearing. When he was gone, James looked critically at his reflection, seeing nothing extraordinary about the slacks at all. They were . . . slacks. Just slacks.

Then he grabbed the pinch of fabric and turned sideways to try to see what the salesman had seen.

Oh. *Oh.*

Well, hello there. He wasn't usually one to get all vain about his appearance, but he couldn't help noticing that the pinches did rather nice things for his ass.

He should definitely stop admiring himself and snap a picture for his sister.

Not of his ass, though.

He took one picture and waited for the salesman to return, thinking he'd take one more with them pinned as well. The salesman came back and knelt at James's feet, and hello, wasn't that a fun and suggestive position? Then he gathered those strategic pinches again and pinned them in place before standing behind James to assess what he'd done. James snapped the picture, trying not to think about the last man who'd stood so close, looming above him and sending electric pulses of awareness zinging through his body.

"What do you think?" the salesman asked, pulling James out of his unwelcome reminiscing.

"I think it looks good. I mean, I think it's supposed to look good." He made an exasperated noise. "Oh, I don't know, I'm not exactly an expert."

The salesman laughed.

"I'm actually going to text some pictures to my sister to get her advice on the whole thing. Is that sad?"

"Sad for me because it means you don't trust my opinion." He put both hands on James's shoulders and gave them a reassuring squeeze. "Kidding! No, it's cool, people do that sort of thing all the time. How about I leave you to do that and bring you back a couple more shirt options?"

"Sounds good." Nodding, James watched in the mirror as the salesman walked away. His mood had taken a sudden dip right at the end there, which he needed to shake himself out of because up until that point he'd been enjoying his almost-not-quite flirtation with the salesman. Paging quickly through the menu on his phone, he fired off a quick text to his sister.

For your approval, J.

The reply came way quicker than he'd have expected from his sickly sister. Hard to imagine she was waiting by the phone for him to text, but maybe she'd been using it to surf Facebook in bed.

Who's the pretty salesman, my sweet?

Oh, *shit.*

Shit. Damn. Fuck! *Why* hadn't he deleted Carson's name from his fucking address book two years ago? James hated the way his breath caught, hated the way he could hear Carson's voice drawling that endearment, hated the way he began to sweat, terror and lust sending his pulse and senses into overdrive in an instant.

As he tried to figure out a way to explain the mistake, or even decide whether to ignore it, his phone vibrated again.

Lose the shirt.

That asshole. James growled at his phone and typed back, *What the hell's wrong with it?*

Isn't your pretty salesman going to come back with others for you to try on? You don't want to make him stand around waiting.

Fuck it all. How could he possibly know that?

Of course he knew. He *always* knew. Just a hint and he knew exactly what James was doing, exactly what he was thinking. He'd known from a single fucking picture that there were *vibes* happening between James and the salesman, after all. Probably getting off on the thought, too.

James was still busy trying to figure out how to put "fuck off" in terms Carson couldn't fail to understand when the salesman returned, three Oxford shirts hanging from his hands.

"Okay, let's try these."

Caught. Trying not to sigh, James started to strip off his shirt. Then his cell phone buzzed again.

Don't bother getting his name.

Don't tell me what to do, you don't own me.

Anymore. James curled his lip at his phone. Stuffing it in his pocket, he smiled brightly at the salesman.

"So, what's your name?"

"Satish." Those full lips curled into a smile as he handed the first shirt over. "I don't wear a name tag because I hate hearing people mangle it."

"Fair enough. Well, I'm James. Pretty hard to mess that up."

He kept expecting his phone to vibrate again, but it was ominously silent as he shrugged into the shirt and buttoned it up. Once again, Satish stepped behind him and grabbed the fabric, drawing it a little more snugly against his torso.

"A size smaller, definitely. And what would you think about a vest? Something that emphasizes the lines of your body instead of obscuring them?"

Oh, Satish, you are most definitely flirting. "What lines? I'm a beanpole—albeit a short one. It's okay to admit it." He flashed Satish a crooked grin in the mirror.

"Not at all," Satish countered smoothly, and set his hand in the lower curve of James's back. "See, right here? There's a dip here. Put a vest on, you'll see it."

His hand felt wonderful, like a lover's. A little possessive.

The phone in James's pocket picked that moment to buzz. "Sorry," he said to Satish and pulled it out.

What's his name, then?

None of your business, James texted back and stuffed his phone away again. He smiled apologetically. "Sorry. Nosy sister."

"Text her about the vest. Go on."

Oh, fuck it all to hell.

Salesman says I should try a vest. Thoughts?

Salesman has good taste. Do it.

Do it. Those two words sent searing need zinging through James's body, making the hairs on the back of his neck stand on end. Like iron shavings lifting toward a magnet. Carson had always been like that. Magnetic. *Electrifying.*

But electricity could kill you if you weren't careful. Best to remember that.

James cleared his throat. "She says the vest is a good idea."

Be sure to send me another picture when you find the right one.

Satish smiled, clearly pleased with the consensus, and gave James another shirt to try on while he went to grab a selection of vests. After he was gone, James pulled his phone out again.

What part of "fuck off" did you not understand two years ago?

You *are the one who sent me the pictures and asked my opinion, my sweet.*

Well, Carson did have him there. Even if the texting today was an accident, that didn't change the fact that James hadn't deleted Carson's name from his phone when they'd broken up.

It would be so easy to clear up the misunderstanding, explain the mistake, and end this. So why the fuck wasn't he doing it?

I have been nothing but appropriate with you, James. James winced. Ouch. It always hurt when he used the name. *You told me you didn't want to see me anymore, so I made myself scarce. I'm a man of my word, and I respect your right to autonomy.*

Well, that's a first. James sighed and fired off another message, glancing up to see if Satish was coming back. *But you're right. You have kept your word. Texted you by accident today.*

Happy accident? Asshole, asshole, asshole. He couldn't go from Domineering Professor Pervert to Sophisticated Cultured Boyfriend just like that. Not now. He couldn't. *Because it was for me. You look good. Clearly you're doing well. I'm glad for you.*

Oh God damn it. James sighed. *Won't know if I'm doing well until Monday. Or whenever they decide on my Ph.D. candidacy I guess.*

Well, you know as part of the department faculty, I can't comment on that, but I'm really pleased you've come so far. I'm proud of you.

Jesus. Why did those words still have any meaning to him?

Maybe because once upon a time, a screwed-up sophomore in danger of flunking out had turned his life around because of them. And in defiance of them. Like it or not, James owed Carson *everything.* God, those first few months, the way Carson had combined sexual and academic discipline . . . It had hurt when he'd failed and it had been heaven when he'd succeeded and he'd come to adore both, in their ways. The whole thing had been absolutely mind-blowing, life-changing, and boy had his grades improved.

Carson had driven him until passing wasn't good enough. He'd made James *excel*.

Funny. Right about now, James could use a little of that reassurance that he could accomplish anything he set his mind to. And having someone to tutor him, guide him, give him a kick in the pants, yeah, all of that.

He swallowed. Considered.

Took the plunge.

Thank you, Professor.

Funny how their relationship had twisted the meanings of completely ordinary academic words. Discipline, of course. Study. Professor. James's mouth was dry just thinking about it. Remembering himself saying "Yes, Professor" and "Thank you, Professor" as he wept with pain from a caning or swallowed a mouthful of foamy cum.

The wait for the next text seemed to take forever.

Go into one of the private changing rooms once your salesman gets back. Tell him you want to try a different pair of slacks. Text me when you've done so.

Shit. *Shit.* Were they doing this? After two fucking years of no contact whatsoever? Were they really doing this again?

James's thumbs seemed to have a mind of their own.

Yes, Professor.

Satish returned with two different vests, and James didn't have to know jack squat about fashion to know they would both look great on him. Which they did, bringing color to his face and making his eyes snap somehow.

"See?" Satish murmured. "In a baggy, formless shirt, you may look like a not-that-short beanpole. But bring everything in, cinch it up a bit? You're David Bowie in his prime. And I must say, the green check in this one brings out your eyes. Well, eye."

David Bowie, indeed. "Looking into my eyes, are you, Satish? And before you ask, yeah, they're natural." One brown eye, one green; James had been born with them, and although they'd gotten him teased as a kid, as an adult they'd proven a surprisingly good icebreaker. In fact, Carson had commented on them on that fateful day he'd summoned James to his office for a talking-to.

"They're great eyes," Satish replied, unabashed. "Does your sister want to see a picture of these, too?"

"Oh!" Shit, James had almost forgotten what he was here for. "Yeah, sure. Also, can I try these with a different pair of slacks?"

"Of course. Just head back to the changeroom you were using before and I'll bring you a couple more options. Careful of the pins, though."

When he was gone, James took another picture and sent it to Carson. A moment later, another message came in.

Explain to me why I never put you in a corset.

James blushed hard. *B/C you aren't into cross-dressing?*

Cheeky. And lying. We both know I'm "into" almost everything.

That was most definitely true. Which, of course, had been their problem. But James didn't want to bring that up just now. Didn't even want to think about it, actually. He ducked into the changeroom and unfastened the fly of the slacks he was wearing.

Try again. People always said you couldn't determine tone from text alone, but James could hear the chastisement loud and clear.

We didn't get a chance, he typed back, perfectly honest. Baring himself to the Professor, yes, that was an old pattern, easy to fall into. *Because of me*, he didn't add.

Much better. You know, it doesn't necessarily have to be accompanied by all the other feminine accoutrements. A corset alone, especially in a specific cut and material, can actually be masculine-leaning-androgynous.

Guess I'll have to take your word for it.

Although I certainly could see myself enjoying you in some panties, too.

James's face burned with shame just at the thought. And yes, this was why they'd broken up—or rather, why James had walked away. Too much, too fast, always pushing the limit. No matter what you gave Carson, he wanted more. More, more, more. Right at the end, James had begun to wonder if he was going to wind up like an orange squeezed to pulp.

Maybe it was time to try something different. Something he hadn't said before. Hadn't known how to say. He'd been so under the spell that by the time things had become more than he could handle, he hadn't known how to refuse.

Too far.

Oh, did my clever little student finally realize that things don't have to be all or nothing, even with me?

Okay, and now he was getting pissed off.

You could have fucking said that at the time.

Asshole.

You're right. I'm sorry. We should have been clearer on boundaries from the start. You were just so wide-eyed and eager, I suppose I got carried away.

James blinked at his phone, gobsmacked. An apology? Fucking hell, *who* was he texting with again?

He was still trying to figure out how to respond without sounding ungracious when Satish knocked on the door.

Satish is back.

Oh, so that's his name. Well, by all means, don't let me keep you.

James opened the door, smiling, forgetting that his fly was open and his pants were hanging halfway down his hips.

Satish's eyebrows lifted, but he was obviously far too good at his job to say anything. He had what looked like four or five pairs of pants over his arm. "I'm afraid all of these are at the very least going to need to be hemmed. There's a couple colors and fabrics here for you to choose from, though. The brown might look nice with that vest you're wearing."

"Cool. Thanks." James, inexplicably bewildered, accepted the stack of clothes with arms that seemed to move of their own accord.

"No problem. There's a little button on the wall there you can ring if you need anything else, but I'll leave you to it for now."

"Yeah. Thanks. Thanks. I promise to buy something." Jeeze, now he was babbling. Time to close the door before things got any more awkward.

With timing so impeccable James could've sworn Carson was psychic, another text arrived the moment he threw the bolt on the door.

You didn't invite him in?

Jesus, Carson. No. He's just trying to do his job.

James took the pile of slacks and hung them on the bar fastened to one of the cubicle's walls. Four altogether. James immediately passed over the first pair. Wool, yuck. Just what he needed: to be doing a massively important presentation with itchy balls.

Oh, very well then, although I can't recall that ever stopping you before.

Flashes of being shoved up against the grimy surface of a handicapped stall with a busboy rutting between his legs while the Professor looked on. Or taking a guy to the seedy backroom of some club while the Professor calmly sipped his drink at the table after giving James his marching orders: *Go fuck that guy and report back when you're done.*

No big deal.

Correction. Never stopped YOU, James replied, but damn the fucking man because a very insistent erection was now poking out of his open fly.

Let's see your other trouser options.

Oh, that asshole. That prick. That dickbag.

I can't, he texted back, wondering if Carson could read the way his teeth were gritted in the words.

Whyever not? He could hear the smoothly arched eyebrow, envision the disingenuous expression.

You know why.

Let me see that, then.

James reached down, taking his cock in hand, literally weighing his options. If he did this, there'd be no going back.

God, he wanted to do this. Carson—striving to please Carson—was like a fucking drug. Carson might take and take and take, but James in turn gave and gave and gave, and got off on it just as much.

If he took that picture, he was going to do anything else Carson demanded of him. And it would be hot. No, not hot. Fucking incendiary. And for an hour or a day or however long, he would once again have that feeling that he could do anything, be anything. Anything wicked, anything superlative. Anything he wanted.

Anything *Carson* wanted.

But the crash after. Oh, God. That was the rub, in Hamlet's words. Because if James was an addict and pleasing Carson a drug, well, the shame that came after, the terror of how far it would go—how far James would let it go—that was the hangover.

And the withdrawals didn't bear thinking of.

Carson waited with what James knew was infinite patience. He wouldn't text again. That was the thing about him: as much as James liked to tell himself that Carson was demanding and pushy and a Bad Influence, he always waited for James to come to *him*. Right from that very first encounter, when things had been an ethical nightmare (what with James being in Carson's class and all), it had been James who'd made the first move.

Of course, back then it had been about trying to fuck his way to a better grade, but the Professor sure had set him straight on that one. Be careful what you wish for, and all that. In the end, he'd *worked* for that grade. And not on his knees.

The kneeling had come after the grade had been earned. A reward for a job well done. By that point, after weeks of study, James had been literally drooling for it. In fact, his mouth was a little wet now, thinking about it. The salt, the sweat, the weight of the Professor's cock on his tongue, the pressure of it slamming down his throat.

He looked himself in the mirror, focused the camera on the jutting shape of his cock tenting his boxers, and snapped the picture.

My. That looks like it needs attention. Certainly enjoying your cage-free existence, aren't you?

Yep.

And yet, he missed that cage, as much as he'd hated it at the time. Contradictions. He was drowning in them.

Surely such a dire emergency justifies a call for assistance.

No. He wasn't going to cross that line. He wasn't Carson's plaything anymore, he was his own man, and playing by his own rules. James took guys like Satish out for coffee and cheesecake before they fucked, and when they did fuck, it was somewhere private. Like James's dorm, or the other guy's apartment, or a hotel room, or the back of a car . . .

Not in a fucking dressing room, watching themselves in the floor-length mirror, trying to muffle their sounds . . .

Fuck.

Carson's reply was terse: *Well then, Mr. Determined-To-Defy-Me, can you take your head out of your arse long enough to show me that pretty cock of yours, or are you going to say no to that without good reason, too?* And fuck James for responding to its tone not with anger, but with, well, wide-eyed eagerness.

He stroked himself through the fabric of his boxers, just his first finger and thumb, hissing at the familiar slide of his foreskin over his shaft. So hard, and yes, he wanted to show Carson, wanted to hear Carson's praise. Missed his praise, all the little compliments he showered James with, and the naughty requests that had flowed from them. He could make James feel sublime and beautiful one second and follow it up with something that made him feel abjectly whorish the next. *My pretty boy, how obedient, I love the look of you hairless, what a lovely cock you have, can you lift your ass for me?*

He was going to come in his shorts before he ever had a chance to comply if he didn't get a grip. Drawing a deep breath, he pulled off the trousers before he jabbed himself with a pin, and then drew his boxers down, tucked them under his cock and balls. Carson had always loved his balls. Loved how tight his sac was, loved the pink seam that bisected his perineum. Just thinking of how much he pleased the man gave James a head rush.

He sent the picture just before another soft knock sounded at the door.

"How's it going in there?"

James jumped, hands flying guiltily from his cock. "Uh, fine! Totally fine! Yeah, just give me a few minutes?"

Which was, of course, the moment Carson replied. Almost in unison, he and Satish asked, *Sure you don't need any help?*

Satish's voice was soft. Inviting. Subtly entreating James to let him in.

No damn it! No! Just because he'd been weak enough to show Carson his dick didn't mean he had to jump right back where their failed relationship had left off.

Failed. That was the operative word. F-A-I-L-E-D.

"No thanks, just in here snapping some pictures." There was no keeping the abject misery out of his voice. If only Satish knew what those pictures were *of.* Not trousers, that was for damn sure.

Satish's voice was a little more distant, a little more proper. Withdrawn. "Oh. Right. Okay. Sorry. I'll leave you to that, then. Call if you need anything."

Fuck. And now Satish thought he'd done something wrong, or that James wasn't interested anymore. Maybe even worried that he'd misread his customer and that his flirting was about to bite him in the ass.

James's phone buzzed, interrupting that particularly depressing train of thought.

Kneel with your back to the mirror. Hand not holding the phone on the back of your neck. You know the proper position.

Yes, James knew, all right, and oh it was so easy to do as he was told, so much easier than the tangled uncertainty Satish represented.

Yes, Professor, he replied, and obeyed. The elastic waistband of his underwear hobbled his thighs. Thank God the changeroom had a door that reached the floor. It would be awkward having to explain to a passerby who could see the bottom six inches of the room, why he was on his knees with his underwear slipping down his legs.

He turned his back to the mirror and took a deep breath. Switched his phone's camera to the front view so he could see his reflection on the screen when he held it up over his shoulder. For a skinny guy, he had a fat little ass, perky, and looking at the curve of his back cinched in the vest Satish had chosen for him made him remember the heat of Satish's hand at the base of his spine. Had Satish been resting his hand there dreaming of cupping James's full ass instead?

Snap went the phone's artificial shutter.

Carson's reply was near instantaneous. *Even lovelier than I remember, my sweet. You're never more gorgeous than when you're on your knees. But so pale. You need somebody to redden you up a bit. How long since you were last spanked?*

Not as long as you hope, James typed back, trying to ignore his cock bobbing between his legs, his shirttails brushing the head, as he remembered the sensation.

Really spanked, James, not little love taps while you're fucking.

Oh. James's face was probably as red as Carson wanted his ass to be, just then.

There had been a time he'd sworn he hated those spankings. And the whippings they'd evolved into. The canings, especially. So well-suited to an old-school academic like Carson, and a disobedient pupil like James had been.

So when had his cock begun to ache and drip at the thought of them?

Since you, he replied. He'd tried the whole BDSM domination thing with other men, but it had never worked out, never even gotten past second base. Nobody compared. That old gay-for-you chestnut came to mind, except in James's case, it was sub-for-you.

Or maybe he could have been submissive to other men, once upon a time, but Carson had ruined him for anybody else.

Poor boy. Would you like me to rectify that?

No question. No hesitation. *Oh yes, please, Professor.*

Easy. So, so very easy to fall off the wagon. Fuck "fall." Take a gleeful nosedive from the wagon, shouting "So long, suckers!" and "Geronimo!" as he plummeted.

Well, I'm sure that in the past years without my guidance, you've racked up plenty of infractions in need of punishment.

A smile twitched at the corner of James's mouth. *Well, if nothing else, I've been masturbating like crazy.*

Oh, yes. At first he'd done it for the sake of defiance, once he'd broken his tether, because the Professor's no-touching-yourself-without-permission rule had been a particularly devious form of torture for a man in his early twenties.

Of course, once the initial anger and rebellion had faded, then he'd done it in yearning, longing for things he hadn't dared admit he missed.

He could practically hear Carson's tutting. *Oh, sweetness, that is a grave offense indeed. You know that pretty cock isn't yours to play with.*

That statement should have pissed him right the fuck off. Half an hour ago, it would have. He wanted that defiance back, but he wanted the pain and the pleasure more. So much more. He was trembling for it; the next picture he took, of his hand wedged between his ass cheeks, one finger rubbing his hole, was blurry and out of focus thanks to the fact that he couldn't keep the fucking camera still.

Too bad you couldn't have accidentally texted me in a grocery store, Carson texted in reply, but didn't elaborate. Not that he needed to; the implication was perfectly clear. And yeah, James was jonesing for him bad enough that he probably would have put a zucchini or cucumber or banana up his ass, if that was what the Professor had commanded.

But obviously that wasn't an option. Carson's next text read, *Lean forward now, face on the floor, ass up. Spread yourself for me. I miss your tight, lovely hole almost as much as you miss my cane.*

James didn't want to do that. Didn't want to take such a humiliating position, especially in a public place. And public place or no, he'd never really liked showing off his asshole. Oh, he liked the pleasure it gave him, sure, had no qualms about being penetrated or even penetrating himself, but that didn't mean he found it attractive, or understood how any other man could, either.

But he did it anyway. Because it was the Professor and the rewards of obeying were almost always worth the mortification.

It took a couple tries to get the picture right, get himself in the frame properly. Looking at the pictures, out-of-focus and cut off as they were, filled him with shame so burning he almost wanted to puke. Bad enough to take the picture, even worse to have to do it over and over again, scrutinizing the results. On the fourth try, though, he managed to get an acceptable shot. His hand, first and second fingers stretched in opposite directions and prying his ass open, and his hole nestled in the V.

So beautiful, my sweet. I know how hard it was for you to do that. Thank you.

And with those words, the shame was almost gone, washed away with pride and delight. He'd pleased the Professor. It never got old. It never faded. Not even when he wished and prayed it would.

When he didn't reply immediately, Carson texted him again.

You don't believe it's beautiful, but it is. It's beautiful for the pleasures it offers me. It's beautiful because it's mine to claim and use and admire.

James was still on his knees, still hunched forward, wrists on the floor as he held his phone in front of his face. *Whenever and wherever you like, Professor.*

Greedy thing, aren't you? the Professor chided. *I think more is required to earn that reward, don't you?*

Anything, he almost texted back, but he managed to salvage at least that much dignity.

Like what? he asked instead.

I think you know what I want from you today, James. I won't ask again. If the answer is still no, I will find a suitable alternative, but you know my first choice. So what will it be?

He'd known. He'd known it would come to this. He'd known Carson wouldn't just let it go. That was why he had been so certain that once he started down this road, he would have to follow it all the way to the end. Because sooner or later, Carson always made him so desperate that he *would* do anything. Even the things he swore he didn't want to do.

He could refuse. Carson wouldn't even be so petty as to end the game entirely if he did. James knew that now, even if he hadn't known it two years ago.

All James had to do was say the word and Carson would switch tacks, seamlessly, without complaint, without attempts at manipulation or punishment. Their play would continue. He'd have James finger himself, maybe, or call him and dirty talk to him within earshot of the other shoppers and Satish, or make him jerk off and come on the mirror, then lick it up again.

But it wouldn't be the same. James would be left with the lingering sense of having *failed* the Professor.

And that, *that* was the most dangerous thing of all. That was the trap, the reason he had never been able to refuse in the past. Not because Carson would chastise him for setting a boundary, but because James couldn't bear the idea of letting him down.

It hadn't been Carson who had pushed him too hard, not entirely. It had been James pushing himself.

He couldn't trust himself to respect his own boundaries. Couldn't trust himself not to jump off a cliff at Carson's say-so, maybe even jump off a cliff without Carson's say-so, but just because that was what James *thought* Carson wanted.

Another text while James hunched there, trying to decide his next move.

James, what's your safeword? Do you remember it?

How could he forget? *Bonnie*, he typed.

Short for Bonnie Prince Charlie, of course, because who could maintain an erection thinking about that catastrophic rebellion and thousands of dead Highlanders?

Well done. I will never hold it against you. You know that.

James's eyelashes fluttered, because they were wet all of a sudden. A tear shook off and rolled down his left cheek. *I know. But it's a moot point now, Professor. I'll do what you want.*

The next text stunned the hell out of him.

Bonnie.

James stared incredulously. What the fuck? Did the Dom get to safeword?

Is it what YOU want? Do you want any of this? If not, we stop now. Stop everything, if you like, or just this particular game.

Carson's hesitation only increased James's determination. Did the old know-it-all asshole really think James didn't know his own mind? Couldn't think for himself? Couldn't handle this? Was afraid of saying no?

But wasn't that what he'd been concerned about—that he *was* afraid to say no? And God, hadn't that been why they'd broken up, because James had thought it over and decided he *couldn't* handle it? Couldn't handle Carson and his games anymore? The problem was that he coerced himself into letting Carson push him too far. So how was he to know what he wanted and what he was agreeing to because he didn't want to refuse and, and, and . . . Christ, he was going in circles.

All right. Yes or no, idiot. Do you want Satish in here or not? Forget Carson. Do *you* want it?

He thought of Satish's full, lovely mouth and that slightly sweet, slightly knowing smile. Satish's hand on his lower back, as if he wanted to lead James somewhere.

Yes. Fuck yes, he wanted it.

Don't stop anything. I don't want to stop anymore. Tell me what to do, you old bastard.

Brat. Give your bollocks a hard tug for your insolence. There went that tone-in-text thing again, because James could have sworn there was a little bit of amused affection in there.

Affection or no, James did as he was told. Gave himself a hard enough yank that fresh tears pricked up in his eyes, then snapped a picture of his pained face as proof. Not that Carson would disbelieve him; after all, the man always, always, always knew when James was lying. But James in turn knew Carson would enjoy the picture for its own sake.

Such lovely lashes. I've missed those tears.

James's reply was full of that unabashed honesty that pain always brought him to. *Me too, strangely enough.*

Well, I'll give you as many as you need to make up for lost time. Later. But first, call your Satish back. Seduce him into the room.

Ok. I'll try.

You'll do more than try. You'll succeed. I know you will, my sweet. I believe in you. Call me before he gets here, and leave the phone on. I want to hear you proposition him. You can hang up after that. No need to compromise the lad's privacy, after all.

Yes, Professor.

Strangely calm, James obeyed.

Once you've ensnared him, get on your knees and suck his cock. He's not to get you off. You're not to touch yourself. You're saving yourself for me now. Once I've had you for myself, perhaps I'll let other men pleasure you again.

A spark of rebellion fired and then faded at that, gone before James had an opportunity to assess why he'd felt it in the first place. He'd think about it later.

The "perhaps" was mostly for show, anyway. Carson would most definitely let James get off with other guys; after all, watching him with another man, even just *knowing* he was with another man—especially if he was dictating the terms of the encounter, like now—never failed to get the Professor off.

Set up according to Carson's instructions, James dialed the phone. He didn't say a word, though. He wasn't ready to hear Carson's voice again. He'd fall apart entirely. Then he pushed the call button on the changeroom wall.

Satish was there in record time. His knuckles rapped on the door politely. "Need a size?" he asked.

"Not exactly," James said, and was surprised by how rough and pitchy his voice was. He unlatched the door. "Come in? Please?"

Just before the door opened, he pulled his underwear back up; probably not a good idea to flash the guy, just in case.

"Um, you didn't like any of the slacks?" Satish asked, giving him an almost furtive once-over, clearly unsure whether or not he was crossing the line.

Oh. Shit. James wasn't wearing any. He was standing here in his fucking underwear and—

Just go with it.

James swallowed hard. Dropped his voice to a whisper, or as close to one as he could manage and still allow Carson to hear him. "I didn't invite you in here because of the slacks. I mean, if . . ."

"A new shirt then, maybe? Or a vest? I found another style in your size if you'd like to try it. Or if you're really not keen on the vest, I found a blazer that might look sharp on you."

Wow. Had he totally misread Satish earlier, or was Satish being shy or playing dumb now? He'd thought his hint was rather blatant. Maybe his aim was off.

God, why was this so fucking *hard*? He was always so confident in his desirability, his ability to seduce, when Carson was around. But without Carson, it was back to the same flailing as always, trying to find the words when it was so much easier to type *25/5'3"/130lbs/uncut/bottom* and send a picture of himself fresh out of the shower and wait for a reply.

"I actually don't need help with clothes at all."

That seemed to work as well as any string of text gibberish. Satish's pupils dilated, black overtaking rich, deep brown and darkening his gaze.

Fuck. He was gorgeous. James would have wanted this without Carson, definitely. But Carson's involvement certainly made it, if not sweeter, then much more volatile.

"Come in?" he asked, stepping back, and Satish tossed a look over his shoulder and followed.

"I can't believe I'm doing this," he said, but he locked the door behind him anyway. "You're lucky my boss knows you need a lot of help, because otherwise this would look seriously suspicious. In fact, it probably still looks seriously suspicious."

"I don't want you to lose your job." Even as he said it, James reached out, wanting to touch that curly black hair. A ringlet fell over Satish's ear, and James's finger slipped into it like it was a wedding band. So soft. It fit him perfectly.

"I appreciate that," Satish murmured. "I swear I don't usually— But— Well. It's not *that* great a job."

James wasn't sure kissing was supposed to have been part of the deal, but there it was: their lips were pressed together, James's hand still tangled in Satish's hair, and it was *good*. Satish tasted good, smelled amazing. James used the opportunity to end the call on his phone before pressing closer. Satish's tongue slid against his, slick and soft and strangely soothing, like a balm rubbed on the rawness Carson had left him with. James felt calmer, less ambivalent. These weren't Carson's desires playing through him. He wasn't a puppet. This was his own.

His desire. And Carson's, and Satish's, in perfect harmony.

His lips tugged and sucked at Satish's, feeling their plushness, the way they softened against his own, the way they seemed to grow even fuller, plumper against his the more he nipped and nibbled and sucked. Imagining those lips wrapped around his cock made him buck and moan into Satish's mouth, which in turn made Satish draw him closer, arms wrapping around his back and tugging him forward until his dick nudged Satish's thigh. Could he come like this, just rubbing against that hard length of muscle and bone? *Should* he? Hadn't he and Carson had a deal? Would he really disobey this early in the game?

"Let me suck you," he said into Satish's mouth, the words as hot and moist as the breath he spoke them with.

Satish nodded, leaning back against the wall of the changeroom, reaching down for his own fly. His eyes were hooded, dazed, and his hand was gentle but insistent as he guided James down. Not like Carson. Not dominant. *Giving*, if anything. Offering himself up for James's desire. Whatever you wanted to call it, Satish knew what he wanted and wasn't afraid to go for it, without being pushy. And *fuck* was that hot.

He wore bright teal briefs that perfectly complemented his skin tone. James found himself sucking on the ridge of Satish's cock through the fabric, darkening the cotton-lycra blend to a color that resembled a tropical ocean. Even through the fabric, James could tell Satish was cut, with a defined vein running up the underside, the kind of feature on a dick that demanded special attention. Lots of licking, oh yes, following that line.

And he had dark hair, too, curly but neat, that came out from underneath his shirt and thickened below his navel. James pressed his nose to it and breathed in, the scent earthy and spicy all at once, so powerful, so masculine and immediate it nearly overshadowed the potency of Carson's words.

He took the head of Satish's cock in his mouth through the fabric, sucking and tonguing, making it wet, so very wet, before he peeled down the briefs and released it.

"Yes," Satish whispered, and James looked up to see him watching attentively. He'd thought maybe Satish would have thrown his head back and given himself over, but no. His eyes were fixed on James, taking in everything James did. His hand was gentle on James's hair, urging him on without demanding anything. "You're so sexy down there."

James answered by licking a slow, broad stripe up the entire length of Satish's dick, tracing that beautiful vein. His eyes rolled up to meet Satish's, never breaking contact. He reveled in it shamelessly, let Satish watch him savoring his cock. Bad haircut or no, he knew he looked fucking gorgeous this way. Maybe this was his destiny, to live on his knees, naked and sucking dick.

Sucking Satish's dick was different from sucking Carson's, though. He didn't feel abject and obedient. But the experience was powerful, nonetheless. New. He had no idea why, but he liked it.

"Please," Satish begged when James's tongue had well and thoroughly wet his dick, leaving it glistening. James's face shone as well, where that spit-coated shaft had brushed his cheeks and jaw. But James wasn't ready, yet, to move on to the next obvious step. Instead, he peeled the underwear down further and turned his attention to Satish's balls. Bigger than his own. Darker. Soft to the touch, and the smell of them when he pressed his face against them—God, it was a powerful drug, and if that made James a pervert, well, he didn't care.

James thought he heard Satish stifle a moan when he began to paint Satish's balls with saliva as he had Satish's cock. The rough hairs there rubbed James's lips as he nuzzled and sucked, one side, then the other. Those hairs began to make a rough, crisp sound the wetter they got.

James didn't care if he was making a mess. He wanted to be messy, wanted to gobble this whole experience up, literally and figuratively. His mouth grew rougher, more urgent. He reached back as far as he could with his tongue, stroking Satish's taint, before drawing away to suck his way back up Satish's dick once more.

"Please," came another breathy whisper, and though James knew what Satish wanted, he still drew it out. He caught the salty-clear drop welling at the slit, then tried to worm the tip of his tongue inside that opening. Wouldn't fit, of course, but the trying was a pleasure all its own.

Satish's hand tightened in James's hair at that, his undemanding acceptance unraveling a bit as he grew desperate. James's hands likewise fisted the fabric over Satish's thighs, holding on, wishing he could drag his nails down Satish's skin.

Maybe next time. James opened his mouth, wrapped his lips around the wide ridge, and slowly sucked Satish in.

A soft sound, a whimper that wanted to be louder but didn't dare, and *fuck* did it sound good. James's hand drifted down into his lap and slipped into the opening of his boxers, where Carson had forbidden it to go. Part of James didn't care, and another part thrilled at the terror and the fierce, heady rush of defiance. He didn't fool himself that Carson wouldn't know—somehow, he'd know, as he always did—but it would be done by then, and worth whatever the cost wound up being. Carson couldn't dictate what James did right now, here with Satish.

He gripped himself and sucked harder. Pressed onward. Slid down that salt-and-spice-and-musk flavored skin until it nudged his soft pallet, forcing him to withdraw. Not that he couldn't take more—Carson had long ago made sure he could—but not yet. Now he just wanted to *taste* and *feel* and let the veins bump along his lips, let the muscle twitch against the flat of his tongue.

"Please. Hurry." A request, not a demand, not a plea. And as much as James wanted to drag this out and make it last, he had to remember that Satish's job was on the line. Carson would probably want him to go slower for that very reason, up the element of risk, but James wouldn't do that.

He couldn't prevent Carson's spirit from infusing every sexual encounter he had; it had been that way since he was twenty. But he could at least keep it from harming Satish any more than it already had the potential to do. He began to move faster, sucking more firmly, throwing into it every trick he'd learned kneeling at Carson's feet.

"G-goodness," Satish sputtered, his voice high and refined, which only increased James's desire. That sort of outburst was no act, it was Satish stripped down to his very purest self: a well-raised, polite man, caught in a sexual game he couldn't even comprehend but unable to resist the lure of James's unapologetic depravity.

And James, once the tempted, now became the tempter, the one drawing an unwitting man into this tangled, terrible, delightful game. But it was *his* game, not Carson's. Not that he had even the slightest interest in dominating or being dominated by Satish, but he still had the ability to determine how this would play out. The power of that was heady, as heady as Satish's smell and taste. Bobbing his head rapidly, his fist around his cock sped up too, chafing a bit but oh the pain was perfect, a reminder of how forbidden this was and of the punishment that was sure to come. Caning? Denial? It didn't matter.

He'd take it and he wouldn't even be sorry for it.

Much.

The tremor in Satish's hands and the tight drawing of his nuts told James the end was hurtling toward them, and he threw himself at it for an unflinching, head-on collision. Carson hadn't specified how this part was supposed to go, but really, even if he had, it wouldn't have made much of a difference. James knew what he wanted, and what he wanted was to swallow a mouthful of Satish's cum, feel it on his tongue, taste it, let it coat the inside of his mouth.

So he sucked. He rolled his gaze upward and tugged at Satish's shirt, just enough to get him to open his eyes to dark-fringed slits. He watched Satish's face and knew Satish was watching back.

He let Satish know how much he loved it, how hungry he was for it. Staring up in pure cock-sucking adoration, James drove himself all the way down, until his lips were wrapped around the base of Satish's cock, until his breath warmed the dark thatch of hair there. Satish made another strangled sound and his eyes clenched shut. Something surged underneath the skin pressed against James's stretched-taut lower lip, and he drew back just in time to let that initial burst erupt across his tongue.

Totally shameless, James jerked himself and watched Satish's face as jet after jet of warm, salty cum coated his extended tongue. A few drops hit his upper lip, but that was fine—better than fine, actually, because in the mirror behind Satish's thigh he could see himself reflected, and he looked so perfect kneeling there with his flushed cock hanging free and his hand a blur of movement and his reddened face wet with tears and drool and Satish's spunk.

When the pulsations stopped, he slid all the way to the root again and let Satish feel the rippling of his throat as he swallowed.

Had he more presence of mind, he would have admired the restraint it took for Satish to limit himself to a few sharp gasps, but there wasn't time for that. The tension in his balls hit the critical stage, and when James's hand twisted and curled around the head of his own cock, there was another rush, another eruption, filling his palm and dripping down his dick. He released Satish's twitching cock, letting it trail spit and slime down his jaw, and panted through his own release, shuddering.

The silence in the aftermath was thunderous. James could practically hear Satish's incredulous *Holy shit, did I actually just do that?* mental litany. But Satish didn't freak out. He was relatively calm as he reached down to stroke James's face before working to right his clothing with hands that still trembled slightly.

James heard a buzz and realized his phone was vibrating. Realized it had been for some time, and he hadn't noticed.

"Your sister?" Satish asked, voice soft as if he didn't really want to speak.

"Um . . . yeah." James looked around for somewhere to wipe his hand and finally grabbed the T-shirt he'd arrived at the store in. "I'll wear this shirt out, if that's okay with you?"

Satish nodded gracefully, some of his composure returning. "Of course."

Hand clean—if somewhat sticky—James checked the message. *Buy all the clothes he's shown you. Make sure he gets a commission worthy of his time.*

Jesus fuck, how much money did Carson think he had? But he was right. Maybe if Satish came out of this with a nice fat sale, his boss wouldn't consider objecting (nor would he wonder about) the amount of time and "individual attention" it had taken.

James smiled up at Satish, trying to look steadier than he felt. His knees ached and some pins that had fallen into the carpet were pricking him just enough to be uncomfortable. Also, he really wasn't used to kneeling like this anymore.

"Ring everything up," he said. "I'll take the whole kit and caboodle."

Satish's eyes bugged out. "What? Are you kidding me? No! I'm not a prostitute."

Ouch. "No, I know you're not. It's just . . . it's to keep your boss off your case. That's all. Promise." To prove it, James reached out and cupped Satish's thigh, stroking tenderly, like a lover instead of a customer. Satish's hand returned to James's sticky face and James turned into the caress. Kissed his palm. Again, like a lover.

Strangely enough, it didn't feel like an act.

"I don't want you in any trouble because of me, okay? So please? Do it? For my peace of mind?" He pushed himself off his knees and staggered when they protested. Satish helped steady him and nodded.

"Okay. Let me take that tag off the shirt you're wearing, and give me those trousers. I'll ring you up while you . . . put yourself in order." A little dimple appeared on one cheek as he smiled.

James smiled back and leaned in, kissing him softly. Lingering in it. It felt good. It felt safe. It felt like something just beginning, not a "Thanks for the quickie and see you later."

He still wanted to take Satish to dinner. Or whatever. Wow.

But it wasn't meant to be, because just then another text came in. *What's taking you so long?*

Satish gathered up the shirts and vests and pants and slipped out of the changeroom.

He's just leaving now. James expected another demand for a picture to come in reply to that, but it didn't. No reply at all. Maybe the game was over, then. He shrugged at himself in the mirror. Time to get dressed and get out of here, he supposed.

Trying to wipe the "just gave a blowjob" mess off his face and make himself presentable, James pulled on his jeans and shoes, then gathered his wadded T-shirt and met Satish at the register. He was looking . . . puzzled.

"Everything okay?" James murmured, leaning casually on the counter while Satish entered the purchases into the register.

"I guess so. I came out to have my manager tell me someone already gave an account number for your purchases and I was to charge it all to that."

Oh, fuck. Fuck no.

James darted a look around the store, trying to find where Carson was lurking, but he could see no sign of him. Bastard probably called it in. Fuck.

What was Carson trying to pull? Was he making a statement about Satish? Was he trying to, as Satish had suggested, make Satish a whore? And if so, why would he bother? James couldn't shake the suspicion that Carson's interest in Satish had an unaccustomed keenness. Why else had he led off asking about Satish? Was it jealousy that James was more interested in a third party than he had ever been in the past? Had Carson realized that James had shut him out of that dressing-room encounter in the end? Out of the action, even out of his mind, at least for a moment. Was he trying to re-exert his preeminence? Remind James who was in charge, who he'd be returning to when all was said and done?

Even now, full of defiance at this latest move, James knew he was still going to end up on his knees before the Professor. They had unfinished business, after all, and God help him, James still *wanted* that. But he couldn't let Carson treat Satish like some random stranger they had used, like they had so many others before.

Satish was different. For the first time, with Satish, James had found the ability to draw the line, to shut out Carson's will and make an encounter about his own will. Satish was a lifeline, keeping James from drowning in Carson's presence and authority. Or at least he had been, in that moment. Who knew if he'd be able to hold up as the storm got fiercer, as all storms were bound to do.

"You okay?" Satish prompted, and James realized he hadn't responded or given an explanation for the account number that had been provided.

"Uh, yeah."

Satish gestured to the stack of clothes neatly folded on the counter. "Is your sister paying for all this? Your parents?"

"What? Uh, no. I'm paying for it." James's own perverse cravings might ensure he couldn't send Carson away again, not yet, maybe not for a long time to come, but he could still issue a satisfying "fuck you" vis-à-vis the pissing match Carson seemed to want to engage Satish in. He fished his credit card out of his wallet, though he could imagine the thin piece of plastic cringing and weeping in terror at what he was about to do to it. "Use this instead. Ignore whatever that was."

Satish's eyebrows went up, but he did as James requested.

Carson was already going to make him pay for his earlier infractions, so why not rack up even more? And really, it couldn't hurt for James to hammer home the message that this time, he would be making a few rules of his own. If there was even going to *be* a this time between him and Carson.

And to that end . . . "When is your next evening free?" James asked as he signed over his next several months' groceries in one flourish.

"Thursday." Satish flashed a sedate smile, clearly okay with what would follow such a leading question.

Far be it for James to disappoint. "Would you go out with me? Dinner, maybe a club if that's your thing? I'd like to see you again."

"I'd like that." Satish held out his hand. "Give me your phone."

James complied, nervously mulling over how much he wanted to disclose to Satish. This was messy. Satish had to know, had to have the ability to opt out of any involvement with James while Carson was still in the picture. And Carson *would* still be in the picture. The floodgates had opened again and there would be no closing them. Not until James decided he'd had enough.

Strange. He was really hoping it wouldn't get to that point again. That this time it would be different, and how fucking warped was that? Was he just greedy, wanting to have his cake and eat it too? Nice, safe, vanilla sex with Satish and . . . *whatever* . . . with Carson? Was he being selfish? Would it be better not to try to involve Satish at all, if he couldn't swear off Carson completely? What the fuck did he think he was doing?

Satish returned his phone, and James decided he wasn't going to do a fucking thing to wipe that sweet smile from his face. He could shelve the bullshit angst for now, think the situation over. At the very least, they could have one pleasant date. Maybe more. Hopefully more. It depended on how Satish reacted to the revelation that there was another presence in James's life.

Whatever happened, though, James was in charge of his own destiny, now. Carson's game, it would always, *always* be Carson's game . . . but from now on, James's rules. He would have a life *outside* the game, a life Carson couldn't touch, couldn't infiltrate. A life that involved more than just being the Professor's *pupil.*

Maybe even a life with Satish in it.

"Thanks," James said. "For everything." Something warmed inside him as Satish let his fingers slide over James's when he handed the credit card back. James drew a deep breath and smiled in return. He could do this. "I'll give you a call, figure out when and where?"

"Sure," Satish replied.

Just let me figure out the how, first.

He wished he could do something more, but with Satish's boss hovering at the next checkout stand, simultaneously scowling over how long the transaction was taking and salivating over how big the sale had been, he really couldn't. So he took his (many) bags and murmured a farewell, heading out to his car.

Another text arrived as James stuffed his bags in the trunk.

I expect you in my office in no more than a half hour. We need to discuss your behavior today.

James stared at it a long moment, weighing his options. There was going to be an accounting for what he'd done, and he'd be lying to himself if he didn't admit he was aching for it, wanted it down to his very marrow. But he wasn't going to let Carson bowl him over, either.

Fine. But we need to talk first.

Very well. But why do I get the feeling that it will be you doing most of the talking?

Well, it's you who'll be doing most of the spanking, so I'd say we're even.

"*Most?*"

Fine. All.

Then you'd best get here soon if we're to have time for talking and spanking. I haven't got all day to wait on you.

James's jaw flexed and his eyes narrowed. That. That right there, Carson expecting him to drop everything and attend him. That was going to have to go, too. Better to draw the line now.

Fine. Maybe tomorrow, then. I'll get back to you.

A long wait, then, sitting behind the wheel of his car. Finally, his phone buzzed one last time.

Call me when you're ready.

James stared at the screen a moment, blowing out a long sigh. He'd almost expected Carson to take offense, despite his assurances that he'd let James set boundaries. But it had worked.

Maybe they could do this after all.

Smiling, James started his car.

Turned out, he was ready now.

Also by Heidi Belleau

Rear Entrance Video series
The Professor's Rule series, with Amelia C. Gormley
The Flesh Cartel, with Rachel Haimowitz
#First Impressions #Second Chances
Blasphemer, Sinner, Saint (Bump in the Night anthology), with
Sam Schooler

With Violetta Vane:
The Druid Stone
Hawaiian Gothic
Mark of the Gladiator

For more visit, www.heidibelleau.com/p/books.html

Also by Amelia C. Gormley

The Professor's Rule series, with Heidi Belleau
Impulse (a novel in three parts)
Book One: Inertia
Book Two: Acceleration
Book Three: Velocity
The Laird's Forbidden Lover

Coming Soon:
Strain
Saugatuck Summer

About the Authors

Heidi Belleau was born and raised in small town New Brunswick, Canada. She now lives in the rugged oil-patch frontier of Northern BC with her husband, an Irish ex-pat whose long work hours in the trades leave her plenty of quiet time to write. She has a degree in history from Simon Fraser University with a concentration in British and Irish studies; much of her work centered on popular culture, oral folklore, and sexuality, but she was known to perplex her professors with non-ironic papers on the historical roots of modern romance novel tropes. (Ask her about Highlanders!) Her writing reflects everything she loves: diverse casts of characters, a sense of history and place, equal parts witty and filthy dialogue, the occasional mythological twist, and most of all, love—in all its weird and wonderful forms. When not writing, you might catch her trying to explain British television to her daughter or sipping a drink at her favorite coffee shop.

Amelia C. Gormley may seem like anyone else. But the truth is she sings in the shower, dances doing laundry, and writes blisteringly hot M/M erotic romance while her five-year-old is in kindergarten. When she's not writing, Amelia single-handedly juggles her husband, her son, their home, and the obstacles of life by turning into an everyday superhero. And that, she supposes, is just like anyone else.

An Inch at a Time

THE PROFESSOR'S RULE, #2

Heidi Belleau
Amelia C. Gormley

James Sheridan is failing history. Luckily, his professor is a rumored pervert, and James isn't too proud to pay for a better grade with his body. Professor Carson lives up to his reputation, but he's not unethical enough to take sexual bribes. What he can offer is some highly unconventional tutoring . . . creative use of a ruler included. The deal? Studying, followed by a "quiz." Wrong answer? Spanking. Right answer? Reward. Ace the final, earn some mindblowing sex. It's harder work than sexual bribery, but it beats the volunteer tutors at the student center. And the better James gets at history, the more he realizes he likes getting answers wrong just as much as getting them right.

Available at http://bit.ly/174R6XB
Ebook ISBN: 978-1-62649-059-8

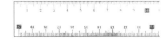

"Are you quite finished?"

Evander Carson gave his student a mocking smile as the kid squirmed in his chair. As far as attempted seductions went, he'd seen far better. It wasn't that James Sheridan was unattractive—far from it, especially with those mesmerizing, mismatched eyes of his—and if he tried, he could probably hold his own long enough to get laid at a club. Still, it was obvious that flirtation wasn't the young man's forte, especially the delicate sort of messages you had to send in a tricky situation such as this.

"I—I beg your pardon?" James slumped, his previously "inviting" fuck-me pose closing off in one shift of his awkward limbs.

"Let me guess. You heard around campus that I'm gay, that I've got—how do they word it politely?—freaky tastes, and thought I wouldn't be discerning enough to mind if you made a rather blatant and frankly clumsy attempt to screw your way into a better grade?" Evander scoffed, shaking his head. "Contrary to salacious rumor, Mr. Sheridan, that's not what I invite students to my office for."

If James turned any redder, he might just spontaneously combust. He looked down at his hands where they twisted in his lap. "I-I'm sorry, that's not what I—"

"Isn't it?" Evander lifted an eyebrow and brought up an information screen on his computer with a couple clicks of his mouse. James Sheridan, age twenty, major undeclared. "Mine isn't the only class you're in danger of failing, and your spring term last year was, well . . . You're already on academic probation. If you don't do well this term, you're likely to be kicked out. Situation like that must have a lad like you pretty desperate."

More miserable squirming. Evander had no idea what James's story was. Perhaps he was struggling and his parents would cut him off if he flunked out of school. Perhaps he was in danger of losing grants or scholarships. Perhaps some terrible personal tragedy had kept him from applying himself academically. Or perhaps he had been partying too much. There were any number of reasons James might be failing.

What was interesting was the method he'd chosen to try to rectify that situation.

And as highly as Evander thought of himself, he wasn't sure if that interest was, well, purely academic . . . or sexual. That level of desperation—let alone forwardness—in a man never failed to excite and intrigue. Even when it was slightly insulting at the same time. Never mind perverted, did the dimwit seriously think he was *that* unethical?

"Tell me, what was your plan for dealing with your other professors?" Evander asked after letting James stew for a moment. "After all, they can't all be reputed perverts like me."

"You were—" Still crimson-faced, James cleared his throat and tried again. "Your class is the only one I didn't think I could turn around this term. History is a lot harder than the others for me."

Evander let himself smile. No denial, not of his play, nor of his opinion of Evander as a known deviant. "All those dates, am I correct?"

"Yeah. Something like that. It's boring. It's too hard to memorize." He huffed like the teenage boy he wasn't anymore.

"Did you ever consider that perhaps the dates aren't important?" Evander leaned back in his seat, mind moving in two equally appealing directions: one-half lofty academic enthusiasm for his subject, the other lizard-like interest in the morsel seated across the desk from him, knobby knees poking out of the holes in his jeans.

"*All the time*, dude." James laughed, and it was hard for Evander to keep himself from laughing along because the honesty was refreshing—if, once again, slightly insulting, this time to his area of study versus his character. "But if they're not, then why are they always on the tests?"

"Who taught your high-school history classes?"

James frowned at the apparent non sequitur. Definitely still a teenager, at least mentally, to be so perplexed by a question answered with a question. Just the type of project Evander most enjoyed. He'd never found it quite as rewarding to work with pupils more suited to academia. There was just something about . . . *awakening* a lad intellectually—among other things. Not that James was stupid. Naive, certainly, but conniving as well, to have come up with this aborted seduction scheme.

"Um—U.S. and world history were taught by the football coach. Western civ was taught by someone else, but I didn't take that one."

"Ah, I see." Evander leaned back in his chair, steepling his fingers over his stomach. "And for a football coach who teaches history but doesn't actually *understand* it, what else besides dates do you think history is composed of?"

"Uh, a steady paycheck?" He laughed at his own joke.

"You're not far off. The dates are on the test because they are all some teachers—especially ones with no genuine interest or love of history—can think to ask. Because they themselves don't understand the intricacies of history, the great tapestry the past forms, stories woven and interwoven and then subject to myriad interpretations and alterations. Perhaps if you could even *begin* to perceive that complexity, you too could realize how truly insignificant—and irrelevant—the task of memorizing dates really is."

James's expression brightened. "You mean your test won't have dates on it?"

Evander resisted the urge to bang his head on the desk.

"Think beyond that, if you please, Mr. Sheridan? I'm saying my test will be both far more challenging—and far more rewarding—than a quiz about significant dates and names could ever be. *If* you want to apply yourself and truly understand what I have to teach you. It won't be easy. You won't just have to memorize a list of facts by rote. You'd have to analyze and understand events that shaped other events that carried ramifications for still more events. You'd have to *think*, not merely regurgitate useless data."

"I feel like you're trying to comfort me, but instead you're just making it worse."

Evander could see the calculations written on James's face, assessing how much time was left in the term and if he could begin to turn the class around and grasp it the way Evander had described. Which was, of course, the perfect moment to make his offer.

"I can help you." One corner of his mouth lifted in a wry smile. "I'm not at all averse to doing some extracurricular tutoring. If you'd be willing to entrust your academic future to the hands of a rumored deviant."

He watched his student's face carefully, searching for—ah, there it was. A flicker of intrigue that went beyond idle curiosity. He could almost hear James's thoughts. *Was* Evander a pervert? What did that even mean? If James consented to be tutored by him, what else might happen?

Evander made no effort to deny the speculation that anything untoward would occur in the course of such tutelage. It wouldn't do to mislead the lad, after all. Evander's reputation wasn't entirely unearned. For that matter, it wasn't even mostly unearned, though it was—*thankfully*—unproven. Rumor alone was not enough to get a tenured professor fired, and certainly none of his students had ever had any cause to complain. He could teach James, of that he had no doubt. And by the end of the term, he would have awoken in his student a passion for far more than history. The spark was there, on both the academic level and the other, even if young Mr. Sheridan didn't realize it yet.

James cleared his throat again, looking both wary and fascinated. Just how naive was the boy, anyway? "Okay."

"Excellent." Evander jotted down an address on a sticky note and reached across the desk to lay it before James. "Be there tonight at eight o'clock sharp. We won't be doing this on campus."

"Okay." James's voice was thick, raspy, as if he couldn't get enough spit together to wet his tongue. But he took the sticky note and stood. Evander politely refrained from commenting on the semi-erection swelling the fly of the lad's jeans. "Thank you, professor."

"You're welcome." Evander dismissed him with a negligent wave of his hand, calling out only once as James's fingers lay on the doorknob. "And Mr. Sheridan?"

"Yes?"

"No underwear."

No underwear.

James blushed in the privacy of his dorm room, where the process of choosing clothing for his tutoring session had just became fraught with all sorts of complications. He'd almost relaxed by the time Professor Carson had laid that last line on him, almost convinced himself that the mixed signals he'd been picking up from Carson had been nothing more than a remnant of the misconception that had led him to make his implicit offer to begin with. He'd actually begun to believe that he wouldn't end up paying for a better grade with his ass after all.

The thought made him cringe. After what he'd done that last week of spring term—or at least what he could remember of it—he'd sworn he'd never pay for anything with his ass again. He was over that sort of behavior, or he was supposed to be. Risen above it. Frankly, this little relapse was something he should probably call his sponsor about.

He'd been relieved when Carson had appeared to see through his scheme, and genuinely grateful for the offer of tutoring. He wasn't sure what had convinced him that he could try to seduce his instructor into giving him a passing grade to begin with, save for campus gossip and the fact that James always seemed to feel Carson watching him during lectures. Oh, Carson addressed the whole hall, yet it felt as though he made direct eye contact with James over and over, far more often than with anyone else.

It was stupid, but something electric crackled and fizzed between them in those moments when their gazes connected. Enough so that when Carson left James a note on his last failing paper saying to make an appointment to meet him during his office hours, James had assumed the purpose to be something other than entirely academic, and he'd decided to try to leverage that in his favor.

And now it turned out he hadn't been far off the mark. Carson just wanted to make sure they didn't do it where they would be caught. Pity. James had actually been starting to buy into all that stuff about how fascinating history could be.

Want to read more of An Inch at a Time?
Visit http://bit.ly/174R6XB

amelia c. GORMLEY

Infected by a deadly virus, Rhys's only hope for survival is simultaneous infection by another strain that might confer prophylactic immunity. But the second strain is sexually transmitted, and its only carriers are the super-soliders from whom the plague originated. To save his life, Rhys reluctantly submits to a period of sexual indenture with the squadron who rescued him, but only with Darius, the squadron leader, does pleasure seem to override the shame.

Worse, the dangers the squadron faces—from violent infectees to even more violent survivors—are putting everyone's life a risk. And with each day that passes, it looks less and less likely that the attempt to protect Rhys from the deadly plague is working. Which means that any day now, Rhys could die—or Darius could be forced to kill Rhys before Rhys kills them all.

Coming February 2014!
Visit www.RiptidePublishing.com for more info.
Ebook ISBN: 978-1-62649-071-0
Paperback ISBN: 978-1-62649-070-3

CHAPTER 1
priorities

Death smelled like old wooden pews whose varnish and cushions had become saturated with acrid layers of dust. It smelled like mildewing carpet rotting from rain that had leaked through a roof he'd never had the skill or resources to repair. The hymnals had long since been used for tinder, but the musty scent of old books—once so comforting but now vaguely nauseating—remained.

It was dim, too. The dust dancing in the speckled sunlight that filtered through the filthy stained glass windows could more accurately be described as sheets rather than motes. In the absence of any other light, it lent the room a dusky quality that would have been beautiful if he hadn't despised it.

Rhys took all this in during what would likely be one of his final heartbeats, as he brandished his shotgun like a bat and scowled at the splintering door.

The moist crunch of the heavy stock smashing in the bones of the revenant's face was a sound he didn't think he'd forget, assuming he lived to remember. He wanted to puke all over the body that fell howling to the floor, its tangled hair streaming and its grime-caked breasts swinging. Even if it—*she*—was trying to eat him, she had once been a person.

Wondering if he should ask God for forgiveness, he bashed the still-struggling body into the aisle runner, which was so dark and dingy a red that, in the faint light, it looked like a river of dried blood down the middle of the chapel. He hoped to snap the revenant's spine or pulverize the brain or at least blind it before the other two—or was it three?—revs he knew were rampaging outside were attracted by the noise. If Father Maurice was to be believed, revenants weren't *actually* undead, despite the name. He'd said that rumor had only started because everyone had assumed the Rot to be fatal without exception. When the virus had mutated and began turning some of its victims into animals, people had panicked and made up wild claims about zombies. But no, the revs were alive, and if they were alive, they could be killed just about any way a living, breathing person could die. They were just strong, insane, and impervious to pain.

Rhys was splattered with blood by the time the revenant stopped thrashing. A drop itched as it chilled and dried on his lip, its weight irritating.

Don't lick. Don't lick. Don't lick.

He supposed it didn't really matter. Even if he managed not to become dinner, he was still a dead man. He had been from the moment he'd breathed the same air as the revenant.

Knowing that made it easier, in a morbidly reassuring way. He had a small knife in his pocket, the faux-ebony handle cracked. It was useless as a weapon, but enough to slit his wrists. Assuming he survived the revs, he might still die a clean death. If he was smart, he'd do it now, before they got through the door.

But then they might still turn and go after Cadence and Caleb.

It was all about priorities, he thought, his chest heaving and his arms aching, staring down with dispassionate curiosity at the caved-in face of the rev he'd killed. He could see that with a remarkable clarity he'd never had before. First, keep the revs from chasing his sister and nephew. Second, take them out and avoid being eaten. Third, kill himself before the Rot set in or he became a revenant. Knowing what to do had never been so easy.

Now, should he stay and wait, or try to bolt? It was taking the other revs longer than Rhys anticipated to come stampeding in. He didn't feel like cowering in the chapel waiting to be eaten, though, so he tried to make a break for it.

It turned out to be a mistake. They caught him in the narrow stone corridor, where he didn't have as much room to swing his makeshift club as he'd had in the chapel. He sprinted down the hallway, gasping desperate breaths, trying to reach the outside door. Then he heard the growling behind him and turned to face their charge. They had fresh blood on their faces and he could only hope it was from Father Maurice or Jacob.

The pair snarled like rabid dogs and stank to high heaven. Their wild manes of tangled hair reeked of oil and dirt. The ones who had once been men had beards even more ragged than the facial hair that grew indifferently in haphazard patches around Rhys's jaw. Clearly hygiene wasn't high on the revenant list of priorities.

Rhys giggled madly. He was losing it, he realized. His senses were aflame, singing; his awareness of *everything* had sharpened to a keen point. His heart raced and his muscles quivered. In those moments before death, he felt more alive than he had in the past seven years. He could almost thank the revenants for smelling so foul, because it made his last breaths into something that actually had an impact.

For one instant, he considered not fighting. Let them kill him. Let his final moment of this *delicious* sensitivity be the excruciating pain of their teeth rending his flesh.

In the end, though, his survival instinct was too strong. He swung his useless shotgun-turned-cudgel with what limited momentum he could muster, knocking the first one back as a spray of blood erupted from a cut on its brow. Its head snapped back toward him, its eyes narrowing in fury. So human and yet so lacking anything resembling humanity.

The other charged him before he had a chance to draw the blood-smeared shotgun back for another blow. It knocked him to the stone floor, driving the breath from his lungs. The club flew from his hands. He managed a lucky blow with his elbow to its throat, winning himself a moment more of existence as it recoiled. Then it pressed down on him again, yellowed teeth snapping.

The world exploded in a series of percussive blasts that bounced off the stone. A hot spray washed over him. In the next second, everything was eerily silent except for the high-pitched ringing in his ears. The revenant above him was still, its weight crushing him until it was hauled off.

His first thought when he opened his eyes was that his final prayer had been answered. He'd died before the revs could begin to eat him. God appeared before him, stern and mighty enough to justify all the fuss people made about Him. His dark face was concerned in a detached sort of way. That made sense, too; he'd never seen any indication that God actually cared for him. He didn't know why God would be wearing camo fatigues or why He had His holy hair pulled back in a ponytail, but who was Rhys to question the Almighty? Instead, he accepted the proffered hand and it pulled him to his feet as though he weighed nothing.

Then things got weird. God patted him down in brisk, hurried thumps as He mouthed something. Then He shouted, and Rhys could *almost* make out the words through the humming in his ears. It was like trying to listen to someone speak underwater. God ripped Rhys's blood-soaked shirt open, trying to jerk it off him. When Rhys stared mutely, unable to answer the questions he couldn't hear, God's expression turned grim and He frowned with merciless pity. He shook His head and His nearly black eyes went cold. Then He turned away from Rhys to gesture to someone.

Then Rhys caught sight of the woman behind him, who held a shotgun in her hands. A startling streak of white threaded through the thick black braid that hung over her shoulder. Muffled and indistinct, as if from a great distance, the man's words pierced the ringing in Rhys's ears.

"He's not answering. He could already be going catatonic if this wasn't his first exposure. Put him out of his misery. We can't take him with us and risk exposing the others."

"No!" His own shouted reply was muted in his own ears. "I'm not infected! At least I wasn't until—" He gestured to the corpses at his feet and at the blood coating his skin.

"Call the others, tell them to bring water! Soap!" The dark-skinned man shouted to his companion, then whirled on Rhys. "There's a wind pump outside. Is there running water here? Showers?"

Rhys began to sprint before he remembered to nod, dashing up the stairs to the communal bathroom. He didn't even bother to strip off his clothes before he turned on the shower and stepped under the frigid spray. The man who'd saved him followed only a step behind, tearing the remnants of Rhys's shirt off with a wet snarl, then swiping the rivulets of crimson water away from his mouth, which Rhys pressed tightly closed.

"You have soap, son?" The dark-skinned man had to repeat it twice, louder the second time, for Rhys to hear.

Rhys shook his head and closed his eyes for good measure. They'd used the last of their supply of soap years ago. He inhaled only when the need for breath was undeniable, afraid of snorting some of the bloody water up his nose. The man began to scrub him with something harsh and pungent smelling. He startled when unknown hands shredded his ratty jeans like they were tissue paper, not bothering to strip the tight, wet denim down his legs.

Only when someone shut off the water and pronounced him clean did he realize that he was naked in the presence of God knew how many people. Blind and still partially deafened, he'd hardly been aware of others coming into the bathroom.

"He's still been exposed," said a low, female voice behind him. Rhys blinked water out of his eyes to get a better look around. The man who'd washed him still stood in the shower stall with him. His fatigues were soaked, and water beaded on his ebony hair. His dark eyes were pitying. He patted Rhys down again, looking between Rhys's fingers, lifting his arms to peer underneath.

"Guess we'll wait and see, then," he said with an edge to his voice.

"Darius—"

He growled. "Don't, Xolani."

She sighed. "There's no harm in taking him with us, at least until he starts to show symptoms. We can keep him isolated, hope for a miracle. There's nothing left here for him anyway."

Take him—?

Rhys pulled away from the strange hands on his body, mustering every ounce of defiance he could, scowling at them. "I'm not going anywhere with a bunch of strangers. Where's my sister?"

Coming February 2014!
Find out more at www.RiptidePublishing.com.

APPLE POLISHER

REAR ENTRANCE VIDEO #1

heidi belleau

Christian Blake dreams of being a kindergarten teacher, but making the grade means maintaining a squeaky clean image: no drinking, no drugs, no swearing, no sex. And definitely no falling for his new roommate—tattooed bad-boy Max, who may or may not be a drug dealer. Most of all, it means no working at a porn store. But Christian's aunt has cancer, and her beloved Rear Entrance Video will go bankrupt if Christian doesn't take over. Christian struggles to find

the impossible balance between his real life and the ideal one he thinks a teacher needs to live . . . all while trying to keep his aunt's dream alive without losing his own.

Available at http://bit.ly/169g0US
Ebook: ISBN: 978-1-62649-034-5
Paperback: ISBN: 978-1-62649-035-2

RIPTIDE PUBLISHING

AVAILABLE IMMEDIATELY: FULLY FURNISHED BEDROOM ON THE DRIVE $325/MONTH
HERITAGE HOME
WALKING DISTANCE FROM SKYTRAIN
UTILITIES INCLUDED
HIGH SPEED INTERBUTTS
MUST HAVE GOOD TASTE IN MUSIC
SHARED KITCHEN/BATHROOM
NOT SOMEBODY'S BASEMENT
YOUR OWN ROOM
RAD ROOMMATES—THERE ARE FOUR OF US (ALL GUYS)
YOU EVEN GET A WINDOW
SMOKING OUTSIDE ONLY / NO PETS
DEPOSIT $175
I'M NOT JOKING ABOUT THE MUSIC THING

t his is all you can afford now, Christian reminded himself. He folded the ad into quarters, then eighths, stuffed it into his back pocket, and stared at the lopsided house in front of him as if he could turn it into something remotely habitable with the power of his mind.

One of his four possible future roommates (all guys) must be a real estate agent in his spare time, because only a real estate agent could call this dilapidated Edwardian fire hazard a "heritage home." Sure, it was *old* enough to be "heritage," but he didn't know where the "home" fit in unless maybe you were a squatter or a feral cat.

Once-white gables sagged under the weight of a flaking shingled roof, and the yellow paint was a sad shadow of its former cheerfulness: dingy, peeling, and crawling with a film of green moss. What wasn't filthy was in disrepair. It should have been condemned.

Christian made his way up the house's weed-strewn front path, hopped the collapsed first stair of the porch and, left off-balance by his acrobatics, fell into the front door. Hopefully a full-body-and-head knock wouldn't sound any different from the inside than the ordinary with-your-knuckles kind.

"Coming!" someone shouted from inside. "Coming! Coming! Just a second!" And there was a clatter like a class of kindergarteners trampling down the stairs, followed by indistinct yelling. (All guys.)

Nobody answered the door, though, so Christian was left to stand around and scrutinize the stained-glass window above his head. Which could use a few replacement panes, a couple hours of elbow grease, and a bottle or two of glass cleaner. He sighed.

This is all you can afford now, he said to himself again. Maybe he'd get it tattooed on himself, like some people got fortifying tattoos like *This too shall pass*, or *Not all who wander are lost*, or that twee *Lord grant me the strength* poem that somebody had been so kind as to lovingly cross-stitch and hang in a place of prominence on the chemotherapy clinic wall.

At last, a series of clicks came from inside the door, four locks in all from top to bottom: the sign of a house broken into with depressing frequency. Christian stood straighter and tried to wipe the expression of disapproval—*this is all you can afford now*—off his face before the door finally opened a crack.

A round Asian face appeared at shoulder height. "Oh, um, hey," the guy said. "Are you Christian? I mean, Christian the name, not Christian the religion. You're not one of those door-to-door Mormon guys or something?"

"No. I mean, yeah. Christian. From Craigslist. Hi." Christian raised a hand, ostensibly as a wave but mostly to try to convince the nervous-looking kid on the other side of the door that he wasn't armed . . . with a weapon *or* a bible, he supposed.

"Cool, okay. I'm Rob. C'mon in, everybody's in the living room waiting." Without opening the door beyond those first two or three inches, he turned and headed down the hallway.

It went against everything Christian had been taught about manners, but he reached down, grabbed the door handle, pushed—

And the door caught on the chain.

"Oh, sorry," Rob said, and just as he slipped the chain, Christian gave the door another push, sending the door and Christian flying into the foyer—well, not the foyer so much as flat into Rob's face.

Rob stumbled back into the entryway, clutching his nose with both hands and cursing a blue streak that seemed seriously at odds with his previously timid demeanour. Christian, pulling his own hair in sheer panic, followed him in and tried to fit apologies in the spaces between the *fuck*s and *shit*s and *motherfucking cocksucker*s.

"What the hell, man!" yelled someone else, barrelling through a side door and into the already crowded front hall. Two more came in on his heels, which made four. (All guys.)

"It was an accident, I swear!" Christian said, putting his hands up and backing toward the front door.

"It was an accident!" mimicked the last of the four, a short, lanky guy with stretched earlobes and a tattoo creeping out from under his white, ribbed tank top.

This was about to get ugly. This was *all he could afford*, and it was about to get ugly. Might as well give up and drop out of school, work two jobs, and hope he could scrape together enough to pay for a place where he could live alone. Maybe a bachelor suite out in Surrey . . .

But it never did get ugly. Rob stepped between his roommates and Christian, arms out, and said in a small voice, "You guys, it really was an accident. I invited him in and then he pushed the door when I was still undoing the chain and he accidentally hit me with the door. Accidentally. So . . ." He took a deep, fortifying breath, like a man about to make high dive. "So calm your fucking tits, *Max*."

The commotion turned to stunned silence. For a second, all they could do was stand and gawk at Rob, who after his outburst had shrunken in on himself, seemingly waiting for the smackdown. But Max just sniffed, spun on his heel, and disappeared through the same side door he'd initially come through.

"Hit him with the door?" the buff roommate in the popped collar asked, falsely light at first, but quickly regaining confidence again. "You sure we need somebody that accident-prone under *this* roof, Noah?" He slapped the one he'd called Noah on the back, wrapped an arm around his shoulders, and steered him into the door Max had gone through.

Just Christian and Rob left, now. Well, them and the yawning chasm of awkwardness hanging between them.

Christian was about to apologize, but Rob beat him to it. "Sorry about that," he said, rubbing at his elbow and tilting his head so his long dark bangs shadowed his eyes. "Those guys are full of shit mostly. Anyway, um, come on, living room's through here. I guess."

You guess? "Wait, so you still want to interview me? I figured—"

"Nah, it was an accident and they know it. Like I said, full of shit." Rob shrugged, turned, and padded into the living room, leaving Christian in the front hall, bewildered and wondering if it was safe to take off his shoes on the old, splintered hardwood.

He did—mostly because he didn't want to add insult to literal injury and he *really did* need this place—and followed them into the living room. They gave him a place of honour in the room's lone ratty old recliner, leaving everyone else to fight for space on the couch, although currently neither Max nor Rob had taken a seat, so not much fighting was going on. Not about the couch, anyway.

And he *had* gotten a splinter for his trouble. A splinter he was currently forcing himself not to pick at, which took a lot more effort and concentration than you'd think, if the fact that he'd missed at least two-thirds of the current conversation was anything to go by.

As far as Christian could tell, it was Max's fault they hadn't even made introductions or asked him a single question. He and Rob were currently locked in some kind of standoff.

"We all talked it over. We all agreed to do this as a group," Rob said in a distressed-bordering-whiny voice that brought out a tinge of a Chinese accent.

"Yeah, well, that was before he wasted ten minutes pounding your face in. I got a thing to be at. An appointment." Max had his arms crossed over his chest, chin tilted up in some kind of watered-down gangster pose. He kept making aborted motions to edge back toward the door, his brightly coloured tattoo shifting over his muscles.

The other roommates spectated in silence while Rob stubbornly soldiered on, the entire time avoiding eye contact and looking a little like he was going to shake to pieces. "Why would you make an appointment for today? You knew we had to do this. You agreed to it. We all ask him a question. We all vote on whether he gets to stay."

"Fine, fine." Max dug around in the back pocket of his skintight jeans and pulled out a crumpled pink Post-it. He unfolded it, held it about three inches from his face, and read aloud in a voice as shaky as a third grader's, "Who is hot-ter: Megan Fox or Zooey Deschanel?"

Seriously? Max looked at him expectantly. *Yes, apparently.* "I guess I hadn't really . . . noticed."

Max tossed up both arms, the Post-it falling from his hand. "There you have it, boys. My vote's 'no.' Can I go now, *Robert?*"

Rob didn't have a chance to answer; Max had already stormed out.

After a second or two, Noah patted the couch cushion beside him. "C'mon, Rob. He wants to be that way, fuck 'im."

Rob smiled a little and went to take his seat. Noah, meanwhile, turned his blue-eyed gaze on Christian. "Sorry about that. If you still want to live here after all that, we might as well just give you the room here and now. I'm *kidding*, Rob. Anyway, I'm Noah. I'm a sous-chef at an Italian restaurant a couple blocks from here. And this is Rob."

Rob nodded like a dashboard bobblehead. "I'm a first year at Emily Carr." He'd returned to his super-soft speaking voice, his accent smoothing out to a flat—if slightly high-pitched—Canadian one again. "I haven't specialized yet but I'm probably gonna go into sculpture."

The roommate sitting on the other side of Noah, a good-looking muscular guy with a nice tan and a hockey player's wings in his shaggy blond hair, raised a hand. "And I'm Austin. SFU athletics. You go there too, right?"

He'd said as much in his email to Rob, which he now knew had probably been printed out, pored over, and carefully categorized before they'd gotten back to him to schedule this meeting.

"Yeah. Christian Blake. Did a degree in Canadian Studies, now I'm applying for PDP—uh, teaching school. I want to be an elementary teacher."

He could see the *nerd* pass across Austin's features at that. His eyes were already glazing over.

"You doing Kinesiology or Communications?" Christian asked, and Austin gave a good-humoured snort.

"Yeah, you're all right, man," Austin said, sitting back into the sunken couch cushions, and at that harmless familiar barb, the tension vanished from the room. Christian couldn't help but let out a sigh of relief.

They asked him about his personal habits (he showered every day but he was quick about it), his schedule (he was an early riser by necessity but he slept like the dead), whether he had any dietary restrictions (nope), if he had a girlfriend (haha, no), whether he drank or smoked or did any drugs.

"No way. PDP is really strict about that stuff. I've heard of people getting kicked out just for having a picture of them drinking a beer on their Facebook, so I quit all that stuff cold turkey. It's just not worth the risk. Oh, but," he amended quickly, "I don't mind if other people do. I mean, it's cool if you guys smoke weed or have parties or whatever. I'm not judgmental."

That seemed to satisfy Austin, who'd been the one to ask the question.

"So why should we pick you?" Noah asked, very seriously. Christian wondered if he was in charge of hiring the kitchen staff where he worked. "Over anybody else who emailed us, I mean. I'm not trying to freak you out, but we're pretty spoiled for choice here."

Christian jiggled his knee, then forced himself to keep still, reminding himself that this was no worse than the torture of his teaching school interview. Not to mention fidgeting made the whole couch shake.

Because this is all I can afford, that familiar nagging voice in his head supplied, *and I don't have anybody left I can depend on and I don't know how I'm going to afford these tuition payments coming up and I don't know if this scholarship money is going to come through and—*

"I always do the dishes?" he tried.

"Sold!" Austin laughed.

Want to read more of Apple Polisher?
Visit http://bit.ly/169g0US